This book belongs to:

....

For Bailey
(with special thanks to Grandnan who was Rebecca's friend)

purplepenguinpublishing
Copyright © 2015 Sally-Anne Tapia-Bowes

FIRST PUBLISHED 2015
ISBN-13: 978-0-9931919-1-6

I'd like to thank Alex for all his hard work in helping me create this text – in memory of Rebecca.

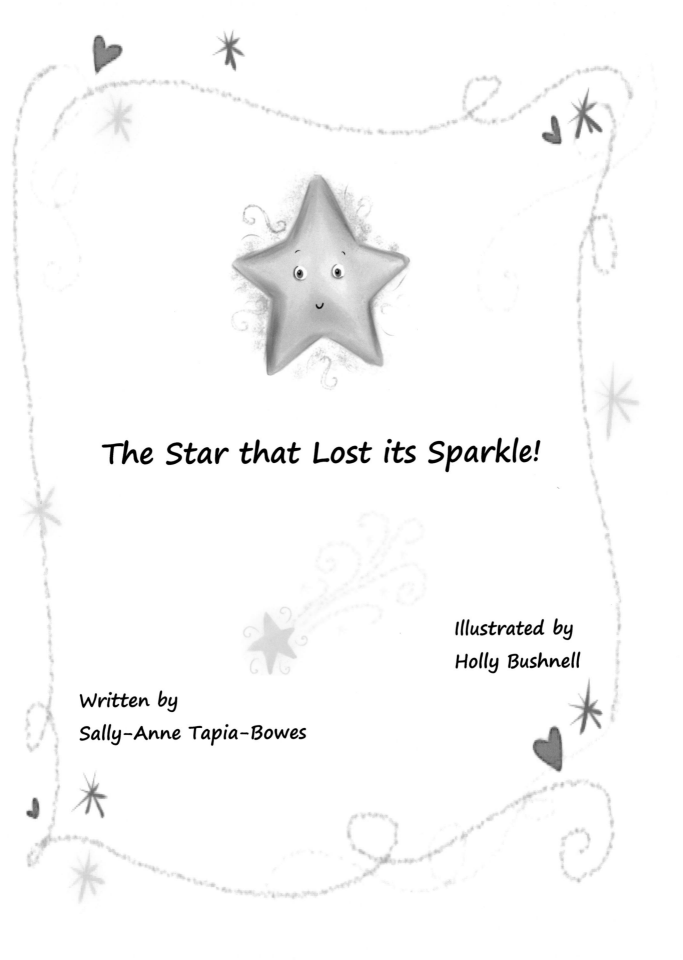

The Star that Lost its Sparkle!

Illustrated by
Holly Bushnell

Written by
Sally-Anne Tapia-Bowes

Sometimes, even in the wide and
gorgeous night sky,
where many moons and stars dance,
and zoom, and zing...
sometimes, there is sadness...
even tears...
even a touch of despair...

Once upon a time,
and thankfully for only a short while,
a tiny and beautiful sky-blue star
actually lost its sparkle!

When the small star got up,
on one fine evening,
his mother pointed it out,
'Bailey, you've lost your sparkle!'
The small star was about to look at
himself in the mirror, just as his father
noticed it too,
'You're looking rather pale. Are you
okay?'
Together all three, stared and glared –
glared and stared, for ever such a long
while: they truly didn't know
what to do.

At the point when the sky-blue
star began to cry round blue tears,
his mother and father,
who had never seen a star lose its
sparkle before,
advised him to shoot over to see
Grandnan, who was wise and kind
and strong
and had been about for a while
and was for sure likely to know
what was to be done.

When the tiny blue star that no
longer sparkled advanced,
Grandnan did not notice.
She did not even notice him enter,
nor when he sat down,
nor when he sneezed rather loudly,
after getting caught in a storm
on the way over.
So the little blue star began to cry.

Grandnan had been listening
intently to the weather report.
She was about to spark a few
cross words about an advancing
meteor storm,
when she suddenly removed her
earphones: she thought she'd
heard a sniff and a snort
followed by a tiny squeal!

When she turned away from
the radio,
she got such a fright!
She just about noticed her little
and only precious grandstar.
What a sorry, sorry sight.
He looked empty and cold
and bleak
and frightened.

Even before the small star
spoke,
Grandnan knew what to do.
She knew what to do right
away!
She signalled for him to move
closer,
closer still.

Grandnan embraced
him and held him.
She held him tight.

She squeezed him
and hugged him,
until he went from cold to
warm...

...then from warm
to hot...

...and then from hot,
to too hot you can let
go of me now!

When Grandnan eventually
let go,
the small sky-blue star
that had lost its sparkle,
quite suddenly ignited
on the spot.

At first, something
sparked up,
right at the centre of
his chest; then little
lightning bolts etched
across his entire body.
Within seconds,
he had lit right up:
bright and light
and luminous.

The small sparkling star was so
happy!
He was so happy,
that he danced and pranced
and leapt about,
much like the cow that jumped
over the moon!

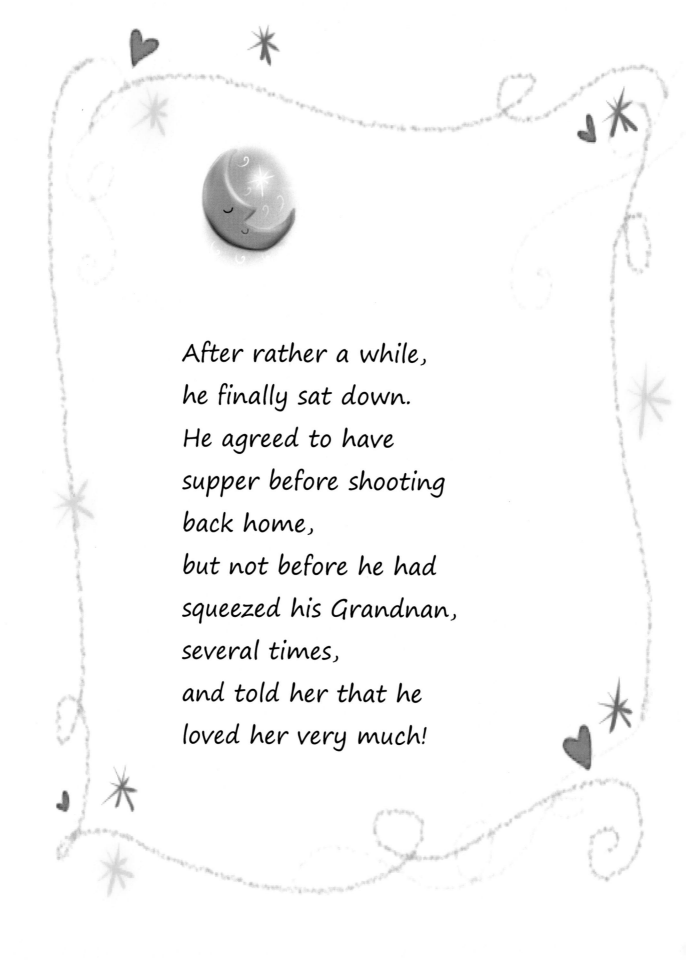

After rather a while,
he finally sat down.
He agreed to have
supper before shooting
back home,
but not before he had
squeezed his Grandnan,
several times,
and told her that he
loved her very much!

STARring:

Bailey

Grandnan

Mum

Dad

70482563R00020

Made in the USA
San Bernardino, CA
02 March 2018